BEARHIDE AND CROW

BEARHIDE
AND CROW

Paul Brett Johnson

Holiday House / New York

In memory of my grandfather
John Commodore Sloane,
who could on occasion stretch the truth.

First Edition

To create the illustrations, the artist photocopied pencil sketches
onto watercolor paper and then surpainted with acrylics.

The text typeface is Raleigh Demibold.

Library of Congress Cataloging-in-Publication Data

Johnson, Paul Brett.
Bearhide and crow / Paul Brett Johnson.–1st ed.
p.   cm.
Summary: After Sam tricks Amos into swapping
a prize-winning gourd for a smelly old bearhide,
Amos decides to give Sam a taste of his own
medicine by negotiating an even more worthless trade.
ISBN 0-8234-1470-1
[I. Barter Fiction.]   I. Title.
PZ7.J6354Be   2000
[Fic]—dc21   99-31000
CIP

AUTHOR'S NOTE

According to a curious bit of Appalachian lore, if you split a crow's tongue, you
can then teach it human speech. I don't know of anyone who has actually put
that notion to the test, nonetheless it makes for amusing speculation.

P. B. J.

They say Amos Dyer was a swapping fool. He was always swapping this for that or that for this. If it wasn't a button for a bucket lid, it was a hat for a horseshoe. And if it wasn't a hat for a horseshoe, it was a jackknife for a jimmy-diddle.

One time Amos's swapping got him in a peck of trouble.
It wasn't long after the Big Swappin' Meet down at Hankins
Meadow. Amos's wife had sent Amos out to the gourd patch.

"Be quick about it," said she. "The water dipper has sprung
a leak and I have to carve a new one."

Amos picked out the biggest, driest gourd he could find.
He shook it till it rattled like a hailstorm on a tin roof. It was
a prize gourd, all right.

About that time Sam Hankins came down the road, kicking up dust. He had a smelly old bearhide in the back end of his pickup. Sam pulled over to see what Amos was up to.

"Fine-looking gourd," said Sam.

"Nell's gourds won a blue ribbon at the County Fair," Amos bragged.

Sam didn't have a bit of use for a gourd, but he figured a blue-ribbon gourd ought to be worth something. So he offered to swap his fly-ridden bearhide. "This here is a magical bearhide," Sam fibbed. "I got it from an old gypsy woman." (That part, at least, was the truth.)

Amos should have figured anything he got from the likes
of Sam Hankins wouldn't be worth chicken teeth. But you
know Amos—couldn't pass up a trade no matter what. Besides,
he thought a bearhide might look awful pretty nailed to the
smokehouse door. So he agreed to swap.

Sam took the gourd and went on his way, laughing to himself.

Amos picked out the second-best gourd in the patch and
went back to the house.

But when Nell saw him coming through the door all covered in that bearhide, she thought it was a ferocious grizzly bear.

She grabbed ahold of a big iron skillet and chased him into
high timber. She might have been chasing him yet, if Amos hadn't
come into some good fortune.

It was getting dusky dark. Amos knew he
would have to let Nell cool down a bit, so he found
himself a dry culvert under the road. He wrapped
up in his bearhide to go to sleep.

About that time two robbers came along. They
stopped to rest right above Amos. Before long they
started talking about a stash of gold they had hid.

"Reckon that gold will be safe?" asked one.

"It'll keep," said the other. "Old Sam Hankins
will never think to look under his rain barrel."

After a bit the robbers went on down the road.
Then Amos got to thinking it might be time to give
Sam Hankins a taste of his own medicine. Yessir,
he would pay Sam a visit come morning.

At sunup Amos was awakened by a peck-peck-pecking noise.
"Peck! Peck! Peck!" It was a big crow, black as midnight, pecking
away at that bearhide.

"Hmmm... A crow is good luck," Amos mused. He grabbed ahold
of the crow and tied a string to one leg so it couldn't fly away. He
threw his bearhide around his shoulders, perched the crow on top
of the bearhide, and started out for Sam Hankins's place.

"Howdy, Amos," said Sam.

"Howdy, Sam," said Amos.

"I see you've still got that bearhide I swapped you."

"Yep. Mighty fine bearhide."

"I guess it draws crows as well as flies," Sam hooted.

"This ain't no ordinary crow, Sam. I split its tongue and learnt it to talk."

"Fancy that, now! What does it say?"

"Sam, this crow allows there's gold buried on your property."

"Haw, haw, haw!" Sam had a good belly laugh. "I'll believe gold when I see it! But you'll have to do the digging. I'll not turn a spade for such nonsense."

So Amos dug a hole under Sam's rain barrel,
and sure enough, there was a sack of gold right
where the robbers had hid it.

Sam's eyes nearly popped out of his skull. "That's
some crow! Don't reckon you would swap it?"

"Nope," said Amos. "I couldn't part with my talking crow. It was just telling me about another stash of gold over in Turkey Holler." Amos put the crow on his shoulder and made like he was leaving.

"What's your hurry?" said Sam. "Sarah Jane is just setting the table. Stick around and have a bite to eat."

"Well, I don't mind if I do," said Amos, so he sat down at the table and had his fill.

When Amos had sopped up the last dab of gravy, Sam said, "Now, about that crow? Tell you what: I'll trade half my gold for it." Being the greedy type, Sam was itching to own Amos's talking crow. If he could figure out where folks had stashed their goods, why, he'd be a rich man in no time.

"You drive a hard bargain, Sam," said Amos. "My wife is out to tan my hide. I need to buy her somethin' pretty, so I reckon I'll swap."

Amos took half the gold and
handed over the crow. He picked
up his bearhide and went on his
way. That wasn't the end of it,
though, not hardly.

It wasn't long till Sam Hankins came tracking Amos.

"Amos Dyer, you sorry swindler! I want my gold back!" said he. "This crow don't speak ary word. It just goes Quaw! Quaw!"

"Why, Sam, that crow talks up a storm. The problem is, you don't understand crow language, that's all."

"Well, I don't understand pig language either. Or squirrel language or frog language. Now give me back my gold!" said Sam.

Amos was thinking fast. "Sam, I can tell you how to learn Crow, same as I did. All you have to do is go to bed every night and cover up with this magical bearhide. Before long you'll be talking Crow as good as anybody."

Sam looked doubtful.

"Sam, you ought to know how powerful this bearhide is. It was yours till you swapped it," said Amos.

Sam started thinking that maybe he had made a mistake giving up that bearhide in the first place. He *had* got it from an old gypsy woman, and gypsies were known to deal in spells and conjuring.

"Look here, Sam," said Amos. "I hate to part with my magical bearhide, but I can see you got the raw end of the bargain. Tell you what, I'll swap this bearhide for the rest of your gold."

And that's how Amos Dyer ended up with all the robbers' gold.

Amos went to the city and bought his wife a whole poke full of pretties and a shiny new aluminum water dipper. He said he was sorry for giving her such a fright, and Nell said she was sorry for taking the iron skillet to him.

Sam Hankins never did learn Crow.